BONNE ANNÉE 1947

The Flying Canoe

Retold by **Roch Carrier**

Illustrated by **Sheldon Cohen**

Translated by **Sheila Fischman**

CHEMIN À VOS RISQUES

DANGER

Tundra Books

So you don't think that a birch bark canoe can fly? As my grandmother used to say, "Crick, crack, crock, youngsters. Tellee, tello, tellum. Now listen hard to what I'm going to tell you. Listen to my story."

This was long before the invention of television or automobiles or airplanes. It was back at the beginning of Canada. Highways hadn't been built yet. Rivers were the roads.

A lot of wood was needed for building houses, barns, and boats. In the fall, once the crops had been harvested, the men left the Beauce to work in the woods. Paddling canoes, they followed the rivers, skipped rapids, portaged from lake to lake until they got to the logging camps in the remote forests. They wouldn't come back until after the ice had melted in the spring.

During those long months of fall and winter, the lumberjacks lived together in a cabin built from tree trunks chinked with moss. Come morning, they often had to break ice on the water in the basin before they could get some of the grime off their faces.

As soon as the sun gave them enough light, they would attack their first tree. They chopped, they lopped off branches, they sawed and stacked wood until darkness fell. And then, bone-weary, they went back to their cabin. Before they fell asleep on their layers of spruce boughs, they had all the thoughts that come to us when we're three hundred miles from those we love.

That year, Baptiste – my grandmother's grandfather – was eleven years old. It was his first time at a logging camp.

Instead of being at school, he was peeling potatoes, frying pancakes, sweeping floors, washing dishes. He had a number of brothers and sisters and he was proud that he could help out his parents, who were poor. But he was just a child. At night, while the men snored loudly, he often sobbed.

Time passed slowly. October . . . November . . . and then, day after day, December. The lumberjacks toiled. They worked themselves into the ground so they wouldn't have the strength to think about those they'd left behind in the Beauce.

Then it was New Year's Eve. At supper, the boss set a small cask of what they called *Jamaica* on the table. He didn't offer Baptiste a drink. Eleven is no age to be drinking rum.

These men didn't have many words. Some of them ventured to tell a joke – there was scant laughter. In the forest up from the Ottawa River, they felt far, far away from the Beauce.

The Boss had had a lot of rum to drink. His head was on the table and he was snoring.

Tom Caribou picked up his fiddle, Ti-Toine Pelchat his accordion, Honoré Beaugrand his mouth-organ. Their music expressed the homesickness they lacked the words to convey.

Baptiste thought about his brothers and sisters. They were at home while he was up here in the woods with the finest lumberjacks in Canada.

Tom Caribou, the eldest of the lumberjacks, had worked in the United States as much as he'd worked in Canada. The men respected him.

"Too hot in here by the stove . . . I'm going outside for a walk." Then, with an insistent wink he said, "Anybody that wants to come along, now's the time!"

He pulled his fur hat onto his head, donned his coonskin coat, tightened a red sash around his belly, and went outside. Without hurrying, five or six men dressed themselves – the way you do when it's winter and you're going to be outside for a long time – and followed him. Though Baptiste was only eleven, he knew that something was up. Dressing himself in a tuque his mother had knitted and a coonskin coat on loan from his father, he went outside to watch the men.

The moon was high and round and beautiful like an orange. Why was Tom Caribou pulling a canoe out from under the bottom branches of a spruce tree? The rivers and lakes were frozen at this time of year. He was handing out paddles to the other men.

"Sit yourselves in your places," he ordered.

And then he spotted my grandmother's grandfather watching them. Tom Caribou didn't sound annoyed when he asked, "You coming along, Baptiste? Been a while since you saw your mamma . . ."

The boy grabbed the paddle Tom Caribou tossed him and took a seat in the canoe. These men feared neither God nor the Devil; they braved storms, bears, wolves. But right now, they were going to take off in a canoe made of birch bark like the ones the Indians made. They were going to fly over forests, cross mountains, fields, towns, and villages. They were going to take flight in the Devil's canoe – the *chasse-galerie!*

How can a canoe fly through the sky like a great wingless bird? There were some who said it was the Devil's magic. Others, that it was a miracle wrought by God.

These travelers, with their rough language, didn't breathe a word. All of them felt a slight shudder in their hearts. On the backs of their necks, some felt the breath of God. Others, the Devil's gasp. They were about to venture into the never-ending night.

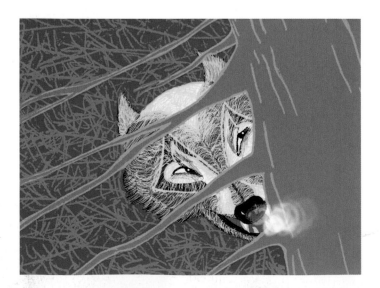

On this New Year's Eve, was it not worth experiencing a little fear so they could kiss their mothers, clasp their fathers' hands, sit around the table with their families, dance the rigadoon, maybe even hold their sweethearts in their arms?

Alone among these bearded men, Baptiste, who had not a hair on his chin, did his best to look brave.

"Hang on tight!" Tom Caribou commanded. "I'm going to say the magic words."

Acabree, acabra, acabram,
Canoe, take us over the mountains!

The canoe, with its eight paddlers, was snatched up like a twig in a hurricane. In fear the men had closed their eyes. When they opened them again they were drifting in a lake of stars. Below them the earth had disappeared.

"I want to go back to the cabin!" let slip Baptiste.

"Jump then!" joked Tom Caribou.

The canoe was now a good three hundred feet in the air. Tom Caribou steered east, in the direction of the Beauce. The air scraped the men's cheeks. The wind combed the fur of their coats and hats. The frost clung to their beards, and their breathing turned it to ice. In rhythm, they paddled with all the strength in their muscular arms. The canoe charged into the night.

The lit-up windows of the first village resembled scattered sparks from a campfire. After all those months in the forest, the lumberjacks were moved at the sight of houses gathered around a church.

Down below, a villager thought that he was dreaming: against the background of the moon he could make out the shadow of a canoe, filled with voyagers, darting across the sky and leaving a trail of sparks like the tail of a comet.

Apprehension gnawed at Baptiste. So high in the air, was the canoe being held up by God's hand or the Devil's? When you're eleven years old you try to hide your fears like a man. The boy paddled as hard as he could.

The snow on the ground was black, but the St. Lawrence River, unmoving in the December ice, was a gleaming road for Tom Caribou and his crew to follow.

Baptiste wished that he hadn't followed the lumberjacks. But if he hadn't come along, he would have regretted that too. After all, a boy has to mix with men if he wants to learn what men know. It was terrifying to be up in the stars with only the thin bark of a canoe beneath his feet. But it was exciting to fly. He was learning how to navigate in the air. One day he'd take his friends from the Beauce on an expedition in his canoe.

It was past eleven o'clock and the voyagers were above the city of Montreal. The windows where lights were burning created a beautiful embroidery of fire. Baptiste had never seen a city: so many houses in one place, so many streets all snarled together. His village had only one street. He would never find his own house in a big city like this.

"Let's get out and have some fun!" suggested Ti-Toine Pelchat, whose throat was parched.

They'd all heard about the tavern where Jos Monferrand, the strongest man in Canada, left the print of his foot in the ceiling. Now that's a place where they'd like to knock back a couple of glasses of *Jamaica*. But Tom Caribou had his hand firmly on his paddle.

"We stop when we get to the Beauce. Not before."

Tom Caribou was not a man to contradict.

The lumberjacks got back to work, thinking about the girls in the Beauce, who were as frisky as the trout in the river and as sweet as maple sugar.

As they neared the church of Notre Dame, the tallest building in Montreal, Tom Caribou gave a powerful thrust of his paddle. The canoe plunged toward the church, and whistled between the two towers that resembled two steep cliffs. The passengers were terrified.

The lingering revellers in the streets wondered if they'd seen a *chasse-galerie* go by. Did it mean that their grandparents' legends were true?

Afraid of crashing into the church, Baptiste had shut his eyes. To hide his fear, he started to sing about the paddles that had brought them up in the air.

> *C'est l'aviron qui nous mène*
> *Qui nous mène*
> *C'est l'aviron*
> *Qui nous mène en haut.*

Some miles away, the canoe met up with a dense cloud – a snowstorm. The snow lashed their faces. Tom Caribou, a fearless captain in this white and furious obscurity, continued to steer toward home.

"D'you think we're lost?" worried the cautious Irish Joe.

"Nope," Tom Caribou reassured him. "Storm or no storm, we sail in a straight line toward the Beauce. Think about your wives. Think about your pretty sweethearts. And keep those paddles moving!"

Whipped up by his words, the lumberjacks made a huge effort to paddle even harder. As they advanced, the storm grew milder against their faces and the snow became fine, nearly invisible. A few houses appeared, scattered along either shore of the St. Lawrence.

At the bow, behind a great wall, stood the city of Quebec, with lights at all the windows. Soon it would be midnight. Everyone was waiting for the New Year.

During the journey, Baptiste had been thinking – he had even made some calculations. To have fire in their stoves, all these houses needed wood. When he turned fourteen, he'd become a lumberjack and travel to the city of Quebec to sell his wood. To Montreal too, where there were more houses and he'd sell even more wood. Then he'd be rich. He would help his poor parents and he too would have a sweetheart waiting for him in the Beauce.

"Let's get out," pleaded pudgy Louis Fréchette. "I've got such a thirst!"

"Right you are," Tom Caribou conceded. "You've all earned a shot of rum. Now me, I've got a lady cousin around here . . . "

"And me," repeated the pudgy Louis Fréchette.

"Me too!" said Irish Joe in English.

"And us," echoed the others.

Obeying Tom Caribou's orders, the canoe descended, ready to alight, grazing the fur hat that sheltered the hairless head of the honorable Speaker of the Legislature. Gently, it touched down behind a cluster of pine trees. The paddlers disembarked; at last, their feet were back on the good, solid earth beneath the snow.

"You wait here for us, Baptiste," said Tom Caribou. "You haven't got the manners to pay our lady cousins a visit."

"Soon as we've had a drink – just one, mind you – we'll be back," promised Louis Fréchette.

"And next stop, the Beauce: women and fiddles and rigadoons!" chanted Ti-Toine Pelchat.

"Just one little glass," repeated Honoré Beaugrand, "then we're off."

They rushed toward the Château St. Louis. With their long beards and their heavy fur coats, they looked more like a family of grumpy bears than guests fit for high society.

All that Baptiste could do was wait. And he waited. Patiently. The clouds glided through the blue night. He followed them with his eyes. Should he explore the city a little? On his own, he'd be liable to get lost. Also, he felt responsible for the canoe. He didn't want to go too far away from it.

The men drank very slowly. The cold bit Baptiste's feet despite his moccasins and his four pairs of socks. And he was tired. As usual, he'd gotten up before the sun to cook the pancakes.

Midnight had probably already passed. If it weren't for this stop, they would already be in the Beauce and he'd be with his parents, his brothers, his sisters, his cousins . . . and the neighbors' daughter, Odélie, who made such pretty music on the accordion. She was eleven years old, like him. Even at that age you'd notice if a young girl had the most beautiful eyes in Canada.

Baptiste was feeling sorry for himself. Could they have forgotten him in the canoe, behind the pine trees? Time itself was frozen like the water in the river. The clouds had stopped moving. He was numb with cold. He dozed a little and dreamed that his canoe was flying away.

What would happen if he repeated the magic words spoken by Tom Caribou?
Acabree, acabra, acabram,
Canoe, take us over the mountains!

The canoe reared up, headed for the moon, and flew in a huge circle above the city of Quebec. Baptiste was dazed but he knew that he had to steer his canoe like a man.

It would be easy to find the Beauce. He just had to follow the river.

Tears came to his eyes when he came upon the gentle valley where he was born and where he had grown up. In the wind he recognized the golden aroma of the *tourtières* that had been baked for the New Year's Eve celebration. Here and there, waves of music rose up above the villages along the river. Baptiste was nearly home. The smoke from the chimneys smelled sweetly of maple.

The street was deserted. The canoe hedgehopped. Through windows covered with frost, Baptiste could see people dancing, and families sitting at their tables. Throwing off sparks, the canoe glided like a comet three feet above the snow-covered ground. In a number of festive houses, people exclaimed, "I swear I just saw the *chasse-galerie!*"

This confession provoked jeers and laughter. "On a night as cold as this, the Devil wouldn't stick his nose outside!"

Finally, Baptiste, my grandmother's grandfather, caught sight of his house at the edge of the village.

"Canoe, slow down!"

His parents had company. A number of sleighs were parked in front of the house. The horses were pawing the ground with impatience. With the wind from the north, and despite their bearskin covers, they thought this party had been going on far too long.

"Canoe, slow down!" Baptiste ordered again.

The canoe hurtled along like a fireball. Baptiste tried to brake using his paddle. He tried all kinds of maneuvers.

"Stop, canoe!" he yelled. "Stop, canoe from hell!"

The canoe was deaf. Baptiste was about to be wrecked. He didn't know the magic formula to moor it. He was desperate.

Stoppitee, stoppitoo, stoppitam,
Stop, canoe, before you get to the mountain!

Like an untamed horse, the canoe leaped.

"If you don't want to stop, canoe, at least slow down a little," he pleaded.

Instead of submitting, the canoe drifted dangerously close to the roof.

A peal of thunder shook the house. The music broke like glass. Thunder in the middle of the winter? This had never happened before. It must have been the wrath of God made manifest; they'd eaten too much, drank too much, danced too much. People rushed outside. The frightened horses shuddered. Everyone peered into the night. Around the moon, all was peaceful.

All at once, a child clutching a paddle fell from the sky and crashed onto the veranda.

"Is that young Baptiste falling out of the sky?"

The canoe, torn to shreds, collapsed onto him.

He couldn't get to his feet; his leg was broken. Luckily Horace Poulin, the finest bonesetter in the Beauce – which is to say in all of Canada – was there to patch him up. Odélie, the young blond neighbor, pressed snow onto his forehead.

Baptiste smiled. "I've come to celebrate the New Year . . ."

Long after these events, Baptiste – my grandmother's grandfather – was still venturing into the woods on snowshoes. Some days he complained about "a bit of a twinge" in his leg. Every time, he blamed it on the fall he'd taken at age eleven, when he'd gone sailing on the *chasse-galerie*.

To Raquel, who has traveled by plane but has yet to fly in a canoe – R.C.

To my wonderful Donna and to my good friends, Lynn Smith-Ary and Zander Ary – S.C.

Author's Note

Imagine that it is New Year's Eve and you are trying to keep warm in a drafty logging cabin deep in the woods near the Gatineau River. One of the stories sure to be told is "La Chasse-galerie," a tale of *voyageurs* who make a pact with the Devil. The story has been told and retold over the years. Perhaps the best-known version was written down by Honoré Beaugrand, who published it in *The Century* in August 1892.

The legend has its roots in European stories involving flying vehicles of one sort or another. When the French crossed the ocean, they brought the story with them. It merged with stories they learned from native people about a flying canoe, and the result is now a unique part of the fabric of French Canada.

Every boy and girl of my age listened to "La Chasse-galerie," a story about a magical flying canoe that carried travelers through distance in the air long before the invention of the airplane. In every family, an uncle, a grandfather, had ventured in that canoe. Years later, when I went fishing in a canoe on the lake, I wished it would carry me to far away countries.

There are many ways to tell "La Chasse-galerie," including an Acadian version in which an axe handle grows long enough for woodsmen to ride. This is my telling of this timeless story.

Text © 2004 by Roch Carrier
Illustrations copyright © 2004 by Sheldon Cohen
English translation copyright © 2004 by Sheila Fischman

Published in Canada by Tundra Books,
481 University Avenue, Toronto, Ontario M5G 2E9

Published in the United States by Tundra Books
of Northern New York,
P.O. Box 1030, Plattsburgh, New York 12901

Library of Congress Control Number: 2004108508

National Library of Canada Cataloguing in Publication

Carrier, Roch, 1937-
[Chasse-galerie. English]
    The flying canoe / Roch Carrier ; illustrations,
Sheldon Cohen ; translation, Sheila Fischman.

Translation of: La chasse-galerie.
Based on La chasse-galerie by Honoré Beaugrand.
For children.
ISBN 0-88776-636-6

    I. Cohen, Sheldon, 1949- II. Fischman, Sheila III.
Title. IV. Title: Fischman, Sheila

PS8505.A77C5413 2004   jC843'.54
C2004-903620-3

We acknowledge the financial support of the Government of Canada through the Book Publishing Industry Development Program and that of the Government of Ontario through the Ontario Media Development Corporation's Ontario Book Initiative. We further acknowledge the support of the Canada Council for the Arts and the Ontario Arts Council for our publishing program.

Medium: Pencil drawings with digital coloring

Printed and bound in Hong Kong, China

1 2 3 4 5 6   09 08 07 06 05 04